D0055692

By Michael Morpurgo

Illustrated by Emma Chichester Clark

EGMONT

We bring stories to life

First published in Great Britain 2009 by Egmont UK Limited
239 Kensington High Street, London W8 6SA

A CIP catalogue record for this title is available from the British Library

ISBN 978 1 4052 3255 5

Printed and bound in Singapore
Colour Reproduction by Dot Gradations Ltd, UK

3 5 7 9 10 8 6 4 2

To Basil and Adrian,
Puppeteers Supreme!
M.M.

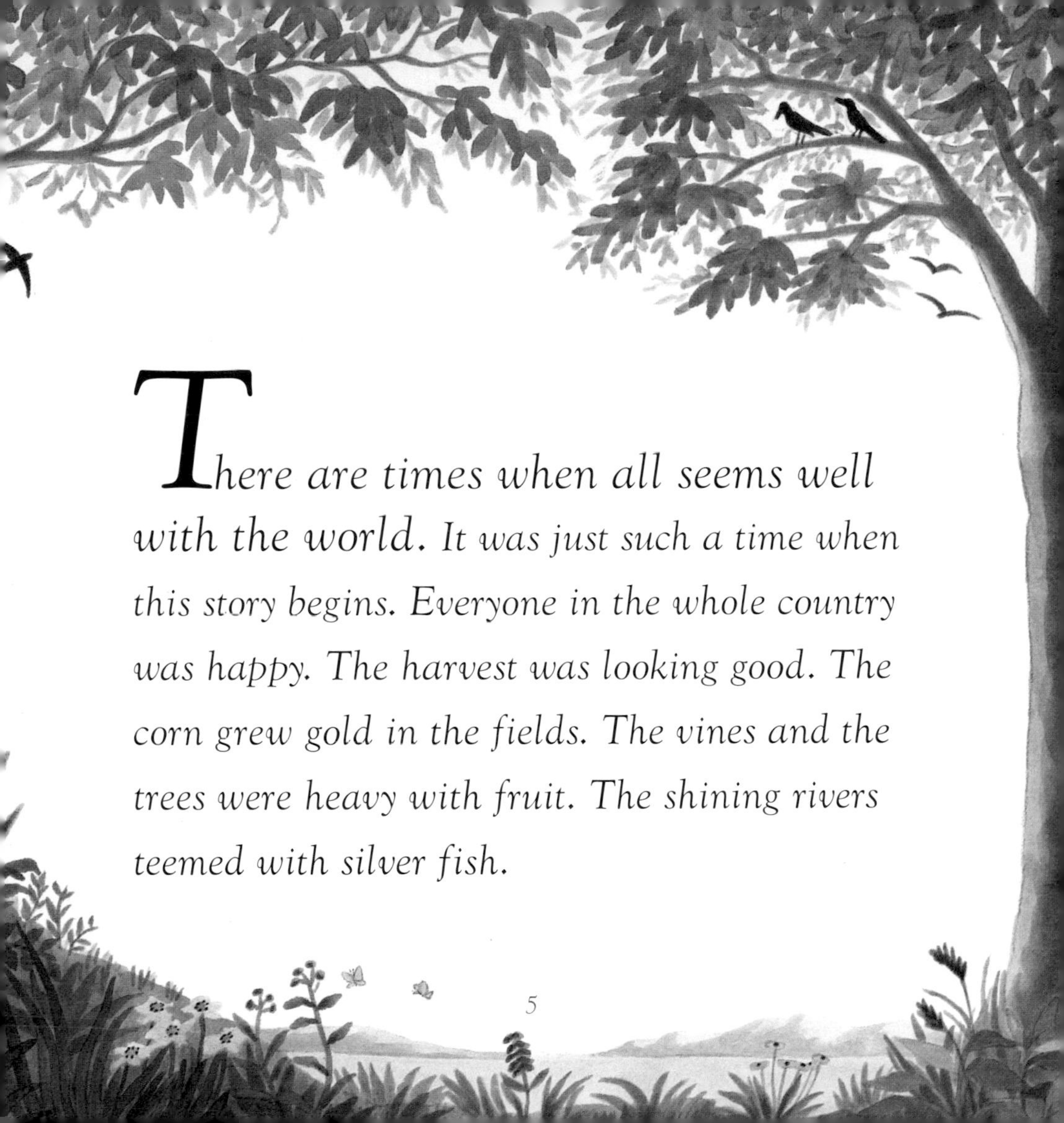

There are times when all seems well with the world. It was just such a time when this story begins. Everyone in the whole country was happy. The harvest was looking good. The corn grew gold in the fields. The vines and the trees were heavy with fruit. The shining rivers teemed with silver fish.

But happiest of all in this lucky land was Prince Frederico. He was more like a brother than a prince to his people, and much loved, which was why everyone was so happy for him when he found at last the Princess of his heart, Princess Serafina. She was a girl of such beauty and kindness that everyone who saw her took her to their heart at once. She only had

to smile and there was joy all around her. She sang, she danced. She only had to laugh and the world laughed with her.

The two married on New Year's Day, and the people went mad with joy. They rang the bells all over the land. They danced in the streets, they rousted and revelled, they feasted and fêted, from morning till night. Never had anyone seen such a happy couple.

But a year or so later, all this had changed. The joy and the gladness had gone. Everyone could see that a great sorrow was settling over the Princess, like a dark shadow.

She never smiled any more, nor laughed any more. She did not sing. She did not dance. She did not speak for days on end. Sometimes she would not even eat. Prince Frederico simply could not understand what had come over his beloved Princess, nor could anyone else. It was a complete mystery.

The light left her eyes. The glow left her cheeks. Every evening, the Princess would sit beside her Prince in the great hall of the palace, not touching her food, speaking to no one. She seemed lost in her own sadness, and could find no way out.

Prince Frederico was desperate to make her happy again. He did all he could to cheer her heart.

At Christmas time, as a token of his love for her, he lavished gifts upon her. Dresses of the finest silk. Rubies and emeralds and sapphires he gave her too, and a pair of white doves that cooed to her from her window when she woke in the mornings. He gave her parakeets and peacocks, meercats and monkeys, and two whippets to stay always by her side and love her faithfully.

But nothing seemed to raise her spirits. No husband could have been more kind and loving than the Prince. He tried his very best to find out why it was, how it was, that she had become so wrapped up in her sorrows.

"We can be happy together again, dearest," he told her. "All will be well, I promise. If only you would just tell me what it is that is troubling you so, then I could help to make things right for you, and make you happy again. Is it something I have done?"

But the Prince's kind words, like all his wonderful gifts, simply left her cold. She turned her head away and kept her silence. Even when he held her in his arms and kissed her fondly, she still seemed far away from him and lost in her sadness. The Prince was heartbroken. There seemed to be nothing whatever he could do to help her. The royal physician visited her every day, but he was as baffled and mystified as everyone else. No medicine he gave her made any difference.

For poor Princess Serafina there was no escape from her sorrows, even in her dreams. All night long she would lie awake. All day long she would sit in her room, ignoring all the food Prince Frederico brought to her, however sweet it smelt, however spicy. A little fruit was all she would eat, and a little water to drink. That was all. She was overwhelmed by sorrow. Maybe after the grey skies of Winter had passed, the Prince thought, maybe then she would be happier.

Spring came at long last, and there was birdsong again, and daffodils danced in the sunshine. But the Princess remained as sad as ever. Prince Frederico was now becoming worried for her life, as was the royal physician.

"She is pining away, my Prince," the physician told him, his eyes full of tears. "She seems to have lost the will to live. If she does not want to live, then there is little I can do, little anyone can do. All I can suggest is that she should get out into the fresh Spring air. Maybe she should go for a ride each day. That might help."

So, the next morning, Prince Frederico took her for a long ride up in the hills, where the air was bright and bracing, where they could look out over the land and see how green and lovely it was under a cloudless blue sky. He put his arm around her.

"Isn't this the most beautiful place on earth, dearest?" he whispered. "It makes you feel good to be alive, doesn't it?"

But Princess Serafina spoke not a word in reply. She gazed out over the cornfields, seeing nothing but emptiness, feeling nothing but loneliness.

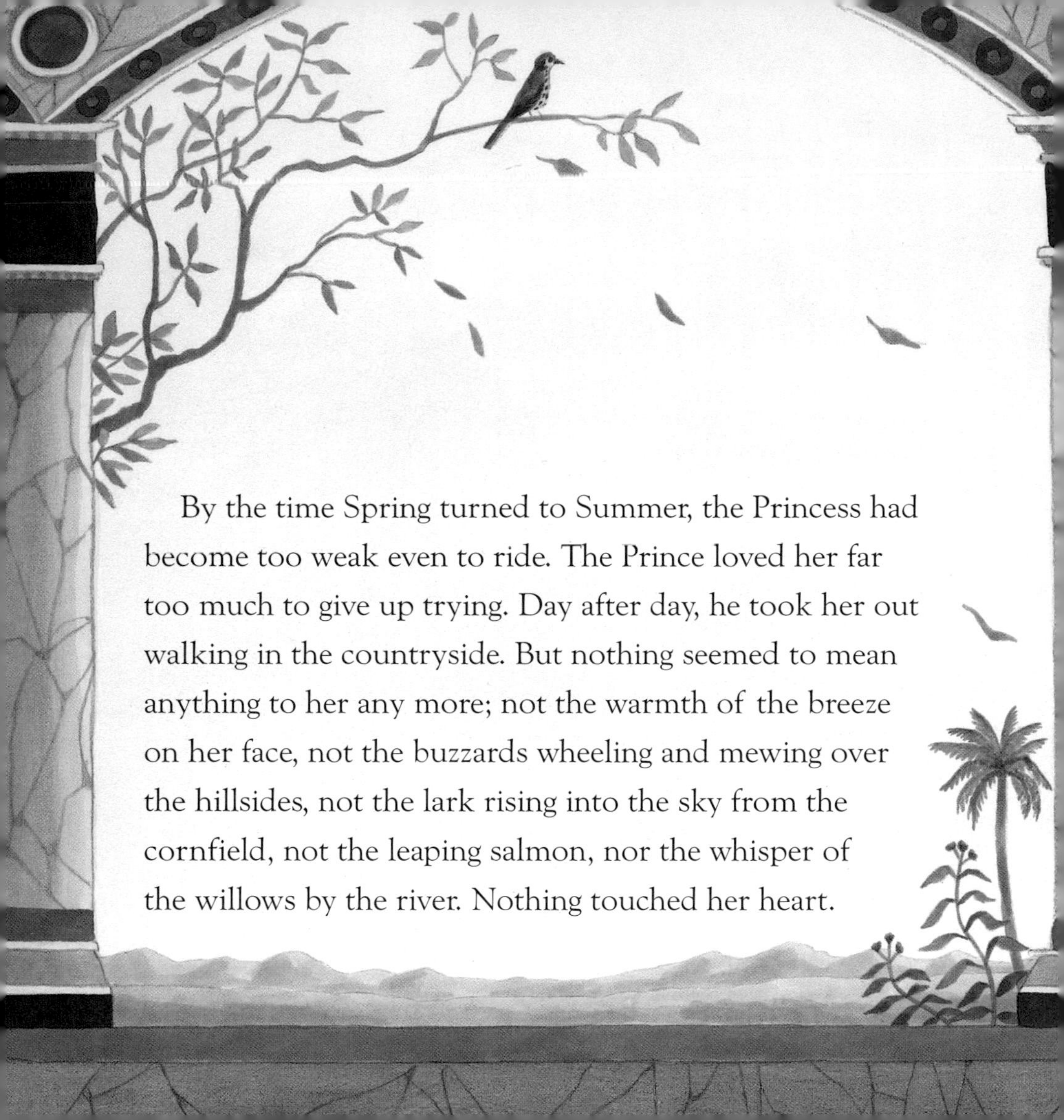

By the time Spring turned to Summer, the Princess had become too weak even to ride. The Prince loved her far too much to give up trying. Day after day, he took her out walking in the countryside. But nothing seemed to mean anything to her any more; not the warmth of the breeze on her face, not the buzzards wheeling and mewing over the hillsides, not the lark rising into the sky from the cornfield, not the leaping salmon, nor the whisper of the willows by the river. Nothing touched her heart.

Now it was Autumn. The Princess was too ill by this time to go out any more for her daily walks with the Prince. Instead he sat with her at her window, holding her hand, hoping and praying for the first sign of a miraculous recovery. None came. Gentle morning mists lay over the water-meadows. Trees glowed red and gold and yellow in the afternoon sun. But the Princess saw no beauty in it, took no joy from it at all.

Winter came in with its whining winds and savage storms. The Prince and Princess sat by the fire now in her room, and he would read her stories through the long dark evenings, even though he could tell she wasn't listening. Then, just a week or so before Christmas it was, the Princess became too weak even to rise from her bed. The royal physician shook his head and told the Prince that he knew of nothing that could save her now, that he must prepare himself for the worst.

"No!" cried the Prince. "She will not die. I will not let her die."

But he feared in his heart of hearts that there was nothing more that he could do.

Inside the palace, and outside too, the news quickly spread that the Princess was close to death, that it could only be a matter of time. The Master of the Prince's Household ordered that all preparations for Christmas were to be stopped, that the holly was to be removed, the tree taken down from the great hall, that there would be no Christmas celebrations that year.

All about him, the Prince saw only sympathy and sadness. Friends and family wept openly. It was more than he could bear. He just wanted to get away from it all. He leapt on to his horse and galloped off into the countryside where he could be alone. He rode and he rode, crying out his grief, shouting it into the wind, into the blinding blizzard that was suddenly swirling all around him. On he rode through the snowstorm, not knowing any more how far he had gone, nor where he was, and not caring much either.

Soon his horse could go no further. The snow was too deep, the wind too harsh. So when the Prince saw the light of a cottage window nearby, he knew he had to stop and seek shelter.

But as he came closer and dismounted from his horse, the Prince realised that it wasn't a cottage at all, but a caravan, a travellers' caravan.

He climbed the steps and knocked on the door.

A smiling young lad opened the door and invited him in at once. He did not appear at all surprised to see him. In fact, it seemed to the Prince that this whole family of travellers must somehow have been expecting him, so generous and immediate, so unquestioning was the warmth of their welcome. They saw to the Prince's horse, stabled her with theirs, made sure she had a good rub-down and a feed. Then they sat the Prince down by the stove and gave him a bowl of piping-hot soup to warm him through. In the glow of the lanterns there were a dozen or more faces watching him as he drank down his soup, old and young, but all of them welcoming. There was no sadness here, only smiles and laughter wherever he looked.

None of them seemed to know who he was. He was simply a stranger they had taken in out of the storm.

All evening he stayed with them as they sang their songs and told their stories. Then the old grandfather, the head of the family, leant forward to speak to the Prince.

"You've heard our songs, stranger, and you've heard our stories. Haven't you got a song you'd like to sing for us? Haven't you got a story you'd like to tell?"

The Prince thought for a while. He had only one story on his mind. "It's about a Prince who lived in a palace, and a beautiful

Princess whom he loved more than life itself, how they had once been so happy, until . . ." And so he told his story.

As he neared the end of his story, one of the children sitting at his feet looked up at him and cried, "And did the Princess die? I don't want her to die."

"Nor do I," said the Prince. "I want my story to have a happy ending. I so want her to live. But, you see, I don't know how to save her from her sadness, how to make her happy again. All of you here seem to be so happy. What's your secret?"

"Oh, that's quite simple," replied the old grandfather, knocking out his pipe on the stove. "We are who we want to be. We're travellers, and we keep travelling on. We just follow the bend in the road. Like everyone, we have our troubles, we have our sadnesses. But we try to keep smiling. That's the most important thing of all, to keep smiling. Now, if that Princess in your story could only smile, then she'd be right as rain, and your story would have a happy ending. I like a happy ending. But there's a strange thing about happy endings, they often make you cry, don't they? Funny that. Very close those two, crying and laughing. We need a bit of both, I reckon." The old grandfather lit up his pipe again before he went on. "This prince of yours, in the story, he loves his princess very much, doesn't he?"

"More than his whole kingdom," said the Prince. "He'd give his whole kingdom to have her happy again."

"Well then, maybe that's just what he'll have to do," said the old man.

The Prince lay awake all night beside the stove, the travelling family sleeping on the floor around him, and all the while he was thinking of everything the old grandfather had said. Outside, the storm was blowing itself out.

By morning, the Prince had made up his mind what must be done to save his beloved Serafina. He ate a hearty breakfast with the family, and thanked all of them for their kindliness from the bottom of his heart. Then, wishing them a happy Christmas, he set spurs to his horse and rode homeward through the snow, hoping and praying all the way that Princess Serafina would be no worse when he got there.

She was no worse, but she was no better either. Prince Frederico knew there was no time to lose. He called his Council together at once.

"Send out messengers into every corner of this land," he told them. "Tell the people that I will give away my whole kingdom, all my titles, lands and property to anyone who is able to make Princess Serafina smile again."

The Council protested loudly at this, but the Prince would hear no argument from them.

"I want it proclaimed that whoever can do this, whoever wishes to win my kingdom, must come here to the palace on Christmas Day – and that is only two days away now." He turned to the Master of the Household. "Meanwhile, we shall make merry throughout the palace, throughout the land, as we always do at Christmas time.

I want there to be no more sadness. I want the Princess to feel the joy of Christmas all around her. I want this palace to be loud with laughter. I want to hear the carols ringing out. I want her to smell all the baking pies and puddings, all the roasting pork and geese. I want everything to be just as it should be. We may be sad, but we must make believe we are glad. Let her know that Christmas is the best of times. Lct her see it, let her hear it."

And so messengers were sent out far and wide, into every valley, into every hamlet and town in the land.

Meanwhile, as the Prince had commanded, every room and hall in the palace was bedecked again for Christmas, and all the festive fun and games began.

By the first light of dawn on Christmas Day, the courtyard of the palace was filled with all manner of jesters and clowns, jugglers and acrobats and contortionists, all in bright and wonderful costumes, all busy rehearsing their acts. There were animals too – elephants from India, ponies from Spain and chimpanzees from Africa.

Inside the great hall, everyone waited for Prince Frederico to appear and, when at last they saw him coming down the staircase carrying Princess Serafina in his arms, they were on their feet and cheering them to the rafters, willing her to be better, longing for her to smile.

How pale she looked, how frail, so frail that many thought she might not live to see in the new year. But everyone there that Christmas Day knew that this would be her last chance, her only hope, and that they had their part to play. They would do all they could to lift her spirits, to let her know how much she was loved. When at last the great doors opened and in came the first of the performers, a clown with a bucket on his head, they all roared with laughter, all of them glancing from time to time at the Princess, hoping for a flicker of a smile.

One after the other, the clowns and jesters came in to do their turns. They cavorted and capered, they tripped and tumbled, but through it all the Princess sat stony-faced. Jugglers and acrobats, the best in the land, cartwheeled and somersaulted around the hall. They amazed and enthralled everyone there, but not the Princess. Everyone howled with laughter at the contortionists' tangled tricks, but not the Princess.

When the elephants came trumpeting in, the chuckling chimpanzees riding on their backs, when the ponies danced and pranced in time to the music, the Princess looked on bemused, unamused, and empty-hearted. As the last of them left, and the great doors closed after them, a silence fell upon the hall, a silence filled with sorrow. Prince Frederico knew, as everyone did, that it was hopeless now, that nothing on Earth could lighten the darkness for the Princess, that she was lost to them for ever.

But just then, slowly, very slowly, one of the great doors groaned open, and a face peered around. A masked face.

"Who are you?" Prince Frederico asked, as into the hall there came a whole troupe of players. They wore no costumes, only masks. Some were older, some were younger, they could see that. And some were women and some men. But all moved lightly on their feet, like dancers. Together, hands joined, they walked the length of the great hall to where the Prince and Princess sat.

"Who are you?" the Prince asked them once again.

"We are a donkey," said one.

"We are a camel," said another.

"We are a cow."

"We are a sheep."

"We are a goat."

"I am a goose."

"And I am a star," a small voice piped up, holding up high a golden star on a long pole. "And we have all made a puppet play for the Princess, a Christmas play, to please her heart." With that, everyone except the child with the star went out again.

Moments later, a goose appeared at the great door, looking imperiously this way and that, as if the palace belonged to him. And then, bold as brass, as if no one else had any right to be there, he waddled into the great hall, stopping to beckon in after him a sheep and a goat and a cow, life-size all of them, and all of them – the goose too – manipulated by masked puppeteers. They breathed such life into their puppets that, very soon, everyone had eyes only for the animals themselves, and the puppeteers became almost invisible. Organised by this bossy goose, who was fast becoming a favourite with the audience, the animals settled down to sleep under the golden star.

A donkey walked in then, a weary-looking donkey. On his back he was carrying a lady who wore a dark cloak about her – everyone knew it was Mary by now, of course. And leading the donkey was Joseph, who helped her down off the donkey, and led her in amongst the sleeping animals, where he sat her down to rest. They sang a carol together then: “Silent night, holy night, all is calm, all is bright.” As they finished singing, Mary opened up her cloak very slowly, and everyone saw there was a baby inside.

A gasp ran around the hall, as everyone saw that the child too was a puppet. His little fists waved in the air. He kicked his legs. He cried out. He gurgled. Suddenly, the Princess was sitting bolt upright, her hand to her mouth, the tears running down her cheeks. Seeing how upset she was, the Prince leapt to his feet at once to stop the play, but before he could do so, she put a hand on his arm.

"Let them go on, dearest," she whispered to him. "I want to see it all, the whole play."

At that moment, in through the great doors there came three camels, masked puppeteers inside them. Living, breathing creatures they were, their heads tossing against their bridles, their tails whisking, chewing and grunting as they came, and each of them ridden by a king bearing gifts.

The goose woke up suddenly, not at all pleased at this unwelcome intrusion. He prowled and hissed around the three kings, head lowered, wings outstretched, as they presented their gifts to Mary and the baby. Then, hissing like a dozen angry snakes, he turned on the camels and chased them off into the night, the three kings running helter-skelter after them. Laughter and clapping filled the hall. The goose took a bow, and then went to have a look at the baby, before settling down again to sleep beside the sheep and the goat and the cow.

Just then, who should come in but several shepherds, looking a bit lost and bewildered. The goose slept on, for the moment. The shepherds found the baby and knelt before him to worship him. Then they sang a carol to him, a lullaby:

"Hush my babe, lie still in slumber,
holy angels guard thy bed,
Sweetest blessings without number,
gently fall upon thy head."

As they sang, the Prince saw the Princess was crying still. Then, like a sudden miracle, she was smiling, smiling through her tears. And by the time the goose woke up, saw the shepherds, and proceeded to chase them, around and around the great hall, she was on her feet and crying again, but with laughter this time.

"I love that goose!" she cried. "I love that goose!"

Everyone was on their feet now, clapping and cheering as the puppeteers came forward to take their bow. The applause went on and on, because everyone could see that the Princess too was clapping and laughing with them, her eyes bright again with life. It was many minutes before the hall had quietened and the Prince could speak.

"You have made my Princess smile," he told the players. "You have made her laugh. So, as I promised, my kingdom is yours."

One by one, players took off their masks, and then the Prince knew them for who they were, that same family of travellers who had sheltered him from the snowstorm, to whom he had told his story.

"We do not want your kingdom," said the old grandfather. "We wanted only to be sure your story had a happy ending, that the Princess could learn to smile again. And now she has. It will soon be the best of times again for her, and for all of you in this happy land."

"Then at least, stay with us a while, stay for our feasting," said the Prince, "so that in some small way I can repay your kindliness and hospitality."

So the players stayed, and feasted, but they would not stay the night. "Travellers," said the old grandfather, as he climbed up into their caravan, "never stay for long. We like to keep travelling on. We just follow the bend in the road. But before we go, we should like to leave you a Christmas gift. Our little goose. We've talked to him about it. He says he's quite happy to live in a palace – just so long as you don't eat him!" And so, leaving the goose behind them, they went on their way into the night. No one knew where they had come from. No one knew where they went. No one ever saw them again.

By Christmas time the next year, Princess Serafina was not only restored to full health and happiness, but she had her own precious baby in her arms, which, of course, was just what the Princess had been longing for all this time. In the play they put on in the great hall that Christmas, the Princess played Mary, and her own child played the baby, kicking his little legs and waving his fists just as he should.

The goose, of course, still insisted on playing the goose. He wasn't the kind of goose you could argue with, everyone knew that. And in his honour – just in case he ever found out – no one in that land ate roast goose at Christmas ever again.